This Book Belongs to

For Ava

First published in Great Britain and in the USA in 2019 by
Otter-Barry Books, Little Orchard, Burley Gate, Herefordshire, HR1 3QS
www.otterbarrybooks.com

ISBN 978-1-910959-32-9

Illustrated with mixed media

Set in Trebuchet

Printed in China

9 8 7 6 5 4 3 2 1

Bruno and Bella
THE SCOOTER

Judy Brown

Otter-Barry BOOKS

One day Bruno got a scooter.

He couldn't wait to try it out.

He was a bit wobbly at first.
"You have to practise," said Bella.

Bruno did. He practised all week.

He practised on
his right leg...

and he practised
on his left leg.

He practised going s l o w l y .

He practised going *fast*.

"I want to go faster," said Bruno.

He climbed the biggest hill he knew.
Bella followed him.

Off Bruno went...

"You're going too fast!"
shouted Bella.

Faster... and *faster*...

Bruno couldn't see where he was going!
He whizzed towards the park.

Bella bounced after him, trying to catch up!

She grabbed the washing line.

"Got you!" said Bella.

But Bruno was heading for the
skateboard ramp!

"Wheeee!" said Bruno.

"Uh oh," said Bella.

SPLASH!

Bella landed in the duck pond.

Bruno wasn't far behind.